MUSEUM MYSTERIES

Museum Mysteries is published by Stone Arch Books
A Capstone Imprint
1710 Roe Crest Drive
North Mankato, MN 56003
www.capstonepub.com

Library of Congress Cataloging-in-Publication Data
Brezenoff, Steven, author.
   The case of the haunted history museum / by Steve Brezenoff ; illustrated by
Lisa K. Weber.
        pages cm. -- (Museum mysteries)

Summary: When a series of accidents and other strange happenings at the Capitol City Natural History Museum lead to rumors that the museum is being haunted by the ghost of a pterosaur, ten-year-old Wilson Kipper and his friends set out to solve the mystery.

ISBN 978-1-4342-9687-0 (library binding) -- ISBN 978-1-4342-9691-7 (pbk.) --
ISBN 978-1-4965-0196-7 (eBook PDF) -- ISBN 978-1-4965-2190-3 (reflowable epub)

1. Natural history museums--Juvenile fiction. 2. Pterosauria--Juvenile fiction. 3. Detective and mystery stories. 4. Best friends--Juvenile fiction. [1. Mystery and detective stories. 2. Natural history museums--Fiction. 3. Museums--Fiction. 4. Pterosaurs--Fiction. 5. Dinosaurs--Fiction. 6. Best friends--Fiction. 7. Friendship--Fiction.] I. Weber, Lisa K., illustrator. II. Title.
PZ7.M47833755 Cah 2015
813.6--dc23   2014026070

Designer: K. Carlson
Editor: A. Deering
Production Specialist: G. Bentdahl

Photo Credits: Shutterstock (vector images, backgrounds, paper textures)

Printed in China
092014   008472RRDS15

The Case of the
HAUNTED HISTORY
MUSEUM

by Steve Brezenoff
Illustrated by Lisa K. Weber

STONE ARCH BOOKS
a capstone imprint

Y TRIBUNE

Pterodactyl...ts
History...um?

Pterodactylus
from over 30
mens, and
those

The back of the crest extended upward into a backward-
curving cone-shaped structure. The crest was com-
posed mainly of long, hard-
ened fibres (twisted together
in a spiral pattern inside the
conical part of the crest), and
covered in scales. In at least

...not
...small,
...present in
...e jaws, with
...and lower hook
...than the teeth that
...ded them.

...mat-
...about
...5 inches)
...unt speci-
...esented by an
...ll). Other "spe-
...once thought to
...er. However, these
...specimens have
...shown to represent ju-
...eniles of Pterodactylus, as
well as its contemporary
relatives Ctenochasma,
Germanodactylus and Gna-
thosaurus.

The skulls of adult Pterodactylus were long and
narrow with about 90 large,
conical teeth. The teeth extended back from the tips of
both jaws, and became
smaller farther away from
the jaw tips (unlike some
relatives, where teeth were
absent in the upper jaw tip
and were relatively uniform
in size). The teeth extended
farther back into the jaw
than in close relatives, as
some were present below
the front of the nasoantor-
bital fenestra, the largest

Pterodactylus, like related
pterosaurs, had a crest on its
skull composed mainly of
soft tissues. In adult Pterodactylus, this crest extended
between the back edge of the
antorbital fenestra (the largest opening in the skull) and
the back of the skull.
The neck was long, and
covered in long, bristle-like

one specimen, the crest had
a short bony base, also se
n related pterosaurs like
Germanodactylus. Solid
crests have only been foun
on large, fully adult spec
mens of Pterodactylus,
dicating that this was a d
play structure that beca
larger and more well de
oped as

Amal Farah

Raining Sam

Wilson Kipper

Clementine Wim

Capitol City Sleuths

Amal Farah
Age: 11
Favorite Museum: Air and Space Museum
Interests: astronomy, space travel, and building models of space ships

Raining Sam
Age: 12
Favorite Museum: American History Museum
Interests: Ojibwe history, culture, and traditions, American history – good and bad

Clementine Wim
Age: 13
Favorite Museum: Art Museum
Interests: painting, sculpting with clay, and anything colorful

Wilson Kipper
Age: 10
Favorite Museum: Natural History Museum
Interests: dinosaurs (especially pterosaurs and herbivores), and building dinosaur models

TABLE OF

CHAPTER 1: New Exhibit..........................11

CHAPTER 2: Haunted..........................25

CHAPTER 3: On the Case...................41

CHAPTER 4: Busted!...........................61

CHAPTER 5: Mr. Moonstar...............75

CONTENTS

CHAPTER 6: Any Suspects?.............83

CHAPTER 7: Ghost Hunters 93

CHAPTER 8: A New Suspect 101

CHAPTER 9: Cracking the Case........111

CHAPTER 1
New Exhibit

Wilson Kipper sat on the big stone bench in front of the Capitol City Museum of Natural History. He held his small tablet computer on his lap, studying a map of the museum as he waited for his friends to arrive.

"You're sure you're okay waiting here for your friends?" his mom, Dr. Carolyn Kipper, asked. "I can stay for a few more minutes if you want."

Wilson glanced at the time in the upper right of the tablet's screen. It was 9:59 a.m. "It's okay," he said. "They'll be here in like thirty seconds."

Wilson's three best friends — Amal Farah, Clementine Wim, and Raining Sam — all had parents who worked at one of the museums in the Capitol City network. Since they got free passes to all of the museums thanks to their parents' positions, the four friends took any chance they could to explore the museums together.

Today they'd be checking out the Natural History Museum. That meant Wilson would be the host, since his mom worked there as a paleontologist. And speaking of that . . .

"Mom, you better get inside," said Wilson. "You're going to be late. I'll be fine." He slid his finger across the screen of his tablet and brought up the museum's website.

"Okay, okay," Dr. Kipper said. "I'll leave you alone."

At that exact moment, three bicycles rolled off the nearby bike trail, heading in the direction of the museum.

"There they are," Wilson said as he clicked off his tablet and stood up to wave at his approaching friends. "Bye, Mom."

Dr. Kipper waved at the cyclists too. Then she ducked into the museum to start her day at work.

Amal's sleek bike screeched to a stop in front of Wilson. Clementine, riding her old three-speed bike, and Raining, on his laid-back beach cruiser, followed behind at a much slower pace.

"Hey, Wilson," Amal said. She rolled her bike to the rack and locked it up securely.

"Hi," said Wilson. "You guys are just in the knick of time. My mom was starting to worry about leaving me out here on my own."

"Is the museum even open yet?" Raining asked as he and Clementine rolled up. Wilson was the only one of his friends who wore a watch.

"It should be opening right now," Wilson said. "Let's get inside. It's the first day of the new exhibit, and I don't want to waste a second."

"What is it?" said Clementine. She pulled off her bike helmet and wiped her brow with the back of her hand.

Wilson grinned. He'd been excited about this exhibit for months — ever since his mom first told him about it. "Pterosaurs," he said.

"Ooh," said Amal. "I know about them. Flying dinosaurs, right?"

"Not exactly," Wilson said as the four friends headed up the steps to the museum. "Pterosaurs weren't dinosaurs. They were flying reptiles that lived during the age of dinosaurs, though. Just like ichthyosaurs weren't actually dinosaurs — they were swimming reptiles."

"Icthyo-whats?" Clementine said, furrowing her brow and looking confused.

Wilson just smiled and shook his head. He loved his friends, but Clementine's mind was usually in a bucket of paint someplace, or sitting in a kiln with her pottery. She didn't know — or care — much about prehistoric beasts.

"Ichthyosaur," Amal said. "It means fish lizard. Right, Wilson?"

Wilson nodded. "Yep," he said as he pushed open the museum's heavy front doors.

The four friends stepped into the huge front chamber. The Natural History Museum was the oldest museum in the Capitol City network, and you could tell the moment you walked in. Everything was wooden and heavy and looked like it had been around for decades.

Right in the front room, which was so big that the Kippers' whole house could probably fit inside, stood the most famous dinosaur skeleton in the museum's collection — the monstrous Allosaurus. It leaned down so that its huge head stuck way out over the velvet rope that surrounded the skeleton. The dinosaur's huge mouth was open like it was about to roar — or eat you.

"Whoa," said Raining, sounding impressed.

Wilson chuckled. "Oh, come on, Raining," he said. "You've seen the Allosaurus model before." He used the word "model" instead of "skeleton" because it was a copy of a skeleton, not a real fossilized skeleton.

Raining shook his head, his mouth hanging open, and pointed up — way up to the high ceiling of the big front room. Wilson looked up too to see what had his friend so impressed.

"Whoa," Wilson echoed when he realized what Raining was pointing at. Hanging there, with its huge wings spread wide and its long neck hanging down, was the new pterosaur model. Its enormous beak was open wide as if it would *kaw* like a giant bird.

"Did you know that this pterosaur was the largest flying animal of all time?" Wilson told his friends. He stared up at the model hanging from chains from the ceiling. "It had a wingspan of up to forty-five feet."

"Wow," said Clementine. "That's pretty amazing."

Wilson nodded. "Its name is pretty amazing too," he said. "Quetzalcoatlus. I read that it was named for the god Quetzalcoatl. The Aztecs in Central America used to worship him. His name meant 'feathered serpent.'"

"I can see why," said Clementine. She stepped around the big Allosaurus podium, gazing up at the Quetzalcoatlus as she walked. "It must have looked like a terrible dragon!"

Wilson thought it was probably way more amazing than some silly dragon from a story, but he didn't say so. Clementine was just like that — always coming up with creative stories.

"Maybe that's where the stories came from," said Amal, walking next to Clementine.

"Don't be silly," said Wilson. "There were no people around when this guy was flying around."

"I mean maybe people found the bones and stuff!" said Amal. "Just because I love space doesn't mean I have my head in the stars all the time!"

The others laughed. Amal was absolutely obsessed with astronomy, which worked out well since her father was the head archivist at the Air and Space Museum.

The four friends walked the whole length of the huge flying creature as the museum began to get crowded. It seemed like a lot of people were excited to see the pterosaur exhibit on its first day.

"Where should we go first?" Clementine asked.

Wilson opened his mouth to say, "To the pterosaur exhibit, of course," but before he could get a word out, there was a loud *snap* from above him.

Someone shouted, "It's falling!"

Wilson looked up — as did everyone else in the museum's front hall — as the largest flying animal to ever exist broke free of its chains and came plummeting toward them.

CHAPTER 2
Haunted

"Look out!" Amal shouted. She threw her arms around Wilson and knocked him out of the way.

Clementine grabbed Raining by the wrist and pulled him toward the wall. All four friends dropped onto their bellies. Around them, other guests screamed and ran.

The Quetzalcoatlus crashed to the ground, smashing the Allosaurus to pieces. Bits of fake bone flew in every direction. All the guests ducked and covered their faces. Little kids cried and held on tight to their grown-ups.

Wilson could feel Amal's arms around him, and he didn't budge till all the noise and shouting was over. It seemed like it went on forever.

A booming voice suddenly cut through the quiet, "Is everyone okay?" It was Lev, the museum's chief of security. "Is anyone hurt?"

Amal stood up, and Wilson got to his feet as well. He took a deep, relieved breath. His friends were all right by him and okay. All the museum visitors were standing in a wide circle around the wreckage. Everyone studied the rubble nervously.

"It looks like everyone is okay," Clemetine said.

"If a little shaken up," said Lev. He put a hand on Wilson's shoulder. "You all right, Wilson?"

Wilson nodded. Then he ducked around Lev and stepped toward the middle of the chamber.

"Don't get too close, please," said Lev. "We don't know if it's safe yet. I don't want anyone getting hurt — especially one of you kids."

"I know," said Wilson. "I'm being careful."

Lev stayed right behind Wilson and put a hand on his shoulder as Wilson stepped up to the wreckage. He crouched down beside it to inspect it. His three friends gathered around the burly security man as well.

"They're both ruined," Wilson said sadly.

Lev pulled off his hat and scratched his head, clicking his tongue. "This has really gotten out of hand," he said.

Wilson stood and looked up at Lev. "What do you mean?" he asked. "What's gotten out of hand?"

"You mean you haven't heard?" Lev said. He leaned down to speak quietly to the kids, but a few other museum guests, clearly curious about how the disaster had happened, crept up closer to eavesdrop. "It's the ghosts."

Wilson squinted up at the security guard. "Ghosts?" he repeated. "Are you serious?"

Lev nodded. "I can't believe your mom didn't mention it to you yet," he whispered. He looked around at the other kids. "None of you have heard about this?"

Raining, Amal, and Clementine all shook their heads.

"Well," Lev whispered, "I don't want this to get around too much, especially to the customers, but — "

"Oh, I think it's too late for that," a woman behind him interrupted. She had two small children with her in a double stroller. "That's exactly why I came down this morning."

"Huh?" said Lev.

A few other visitors standing nearby nodded eagerly. "We all heard about the haunting," said a man visiting with a large group of adults. "We came down to check it out for ourselves."

Lev stood up straight and put his fists on his hips. "I guess word's gotten out," he said, shaking his head ruefully.

"How about you let us in on it?" said Amal.

"Yeah," said Clementine. "I love ghost stories."

Wilson rolled his eyes. Clementine was always falling for hokey stuff like ghosts and superstitions and mind readers. To Wilson, it was all just silly stories covering up the scientific truth. Still, he wanted to hear what had been happening at the museum — and why everyone seemed to be so convinced that the place was haunted.

"It all started last week," Lev told them. "I think it was Wednesday. First the model Velociraptor walked to the cafeteria."

"You saw it walking?!" said Amal, eyes wide.

Lev shook his head. "No," he said. "No one actually *saw* it walking. But it was in its usual spot on Tuesday night. When I unlocked the cafeteria on Wednesday morning, it was there, standing in line at the cash register."

Then it probably didn't walk there on its own, Wilson thought.

"What else?" Clementine asked, leaning closer.

"When I was locking up on Wednesday night, the lights on the third floor, the ones across the courtyard from here, flickered on and off for a few minutes," Lev said. "It sure spooked me."

The security guard gestured toward the huge windows that looked out on the courtyard. Past the models of mammoths and saber-tooth cats and giant sloths, Wilson could see the office, laboratory, and archives area of the museum. Most guests never went to those areas of course, but Wilson had seen it all — his mom had showed him around on his first visit.

"Anyone could have done that," Amal said, crossing her arms.

Wilson was glad she was skeptical of Lev's ghost talk too. *At least I'm not the only one*, he thought.

"I thought that too, but there's no one else in the museum at that hour," Lev said. "It's just me and the security staff."

"Hmm . . ." said Amal.

Wilson still wasn't convinced. "Anything else?" he asked. "So far, all this stuff can be pretty easily explained."

"Maybe," said Lev. "But I'm not finished. On Friday morning, Nancy from the cleaning staff and I were the first people here. The sun was hardly up. I unlocked the door, and we both saw it."

"Saw what?" Clementine asked breathlessly. She leaned forward, clearly excited about a good ghost sighting.

Lev's eyes went wide. "A huge, shadowy figure," he said. "It looked like it had wings as big as an airplane! And it was floating straight toward us, right in this room!"

"Um," said Wilson, "wasn't that the Quetzalcoatlus? The one that just came crashing down?"

Lev shook his head. "That wasn't installed until Sunday afternoon," he said. "They put it up when the pterosaur exhibit was being set up."

"I bet it's the angry spirit of a long-dead pterodactyl," said Clementine, her eyes wide and her voice pitched with excitement. "She's probably back to haunt the museum because they stole the bones of her children!"

Wilson resisted the urge to laugh at Clementine's crazy suggestion. "You actually *saw* a huge flying animal?" he asked Lev.

"Well . . . no," Lev admitted. "We saw its shadow, though." He pointed at the curved wall over the entrance to the ichthyosaur wing, where a giant banner now hung announcing the new pterosaur exhibit. "Right there. It took up the whole wall, so it must have come from something pretty huge."

"Or it was a huge ghost," Clementine said. "Ghosts could look like shadows, I bet."

Lev nodded eagerly.

Wilson was glad when the silly ghost talk was interrupted by a stern shout: "Everyone back away from the area, please!"

Mr. Collini, the museum's director, stomped into the room. He shoved past curious bystanders and came to a stop in front of Lev. "How did this happen?" he demanded.

"All the cables snapped," Lev said, shaking his head. "Practically at the same time."

"Hmm," said Mr. Collini. He stepped carefully into the rubble and found one of the cables that had been holding up the Quetzalcoatlus. "How could that have happened?"

Mr. Collini pulled the length of cable till he found its end. Wilson caught a glimpse. The end looked too neat to have snapped.

"Isn't it obvious?" said Lev. "The ghosts."

Mr. Collini sighed and stood back up. He dug the velvet rope and metal posts, some of which had fallen over, from beneath the mess of model bones. Lev helped him set the barrier back up around the wreckage.

While they worked, Wilson took the opportunity to whisper to his friends. "Did you see the end of the cable? It was clean, not frayed."

"Like someone cut it?" Clementine asked.

Wilson nodded. "Exactly."

"So either there's a ghost in the museum with a pair of cable clippers in its pocket," said Amal, "or this wasn't the work of any ghost at all."

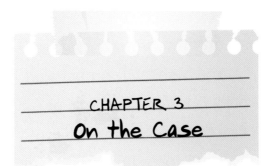

CHAPTER 3
On the Case

Later that day, after the mess in the museum's front hall had finally been contained, Wilson, Clementine, Raining, and Amal sat on the ragged old couch in Dr. Kipper's office.

The museum had been closed to the public for the rest of the day as a result of the accident, but the four friends were allowed to remain inside — as long as they stayed out of the way.

"I just can't imagine what's come over everyone here," Dr. Kipper said, pacing back and forth in front of them. "Practically every member of the museum's staff, including a handful of actual scientists, is *convinced* we're dealing with ghosts."

"It's crazy," Wilson agreed, shaking his head.

"Madness," Amal said.

"So weird," said Raining.

"Well, I like it," said Clementine, sounding energized. "It's exciting. Thanks for letting us hang out in your office, Dr. Kipper."

"You're very welcome, Clementine," Dr. Kipper said. "As long as the museum is closed to guests, you're welcome to hang out here."

Just then, the phone on Dr. Kipper's desk started ringing loudly, and she quickly grabbed it. "Paleontology, this is Dr. Kipper speaking," she said. "Mmhm . . . wait, what? Are you kidding?" She sighed heavily. "Fine. I'll be there in five minutes."

Wilson's mother hung up and sighed again. "This has gotten even more nuts," she said, running her hand over her close-cut curly hair. "Mr. Collini has called in the experts."

"You mean like a detective?" Raining asked.

"The police?" Amal said.

"The MythBusters?" Wilson guessed, crossing his arms.

Dr. Kipper shook her head. "Worse," she said. "Ghost hunters — including a psychic."

At that, Clementine sat straight up. "Ooh," she said. "Can we watch them ghost hunt?"

"I don't think so," said Dr. Kipper firmly. "You kids need to stay in here. I, on the other hand, have to go meet with the psychic."

"What?" said Wilson. "Why?"

"Everyone on staff is required to," his mom told him. "I guess it's Mr. Collini's orders."

"But what about us?" said Wilson. "We have to just sit here?"

Dr. Kipper grabbed her blazer from the back of her desk chair and slipped it on. "I'd stay out of sight if I were you," she said. "If the ghost hunters see you, they'll either make you talk to their psychic or they'll think you're a ghost."

"Or zap us or something," Raining muttered.

Dr. Kipper laughed. "I don't think we have to worry about that, but it's better for you to stay here. Just in case." With that, she left the office, closing the door behind her.

"Well," said Amal, standing up, "we're obviously not staying here when there's a mystery to solve."

The others stood up too. "Or a ghost to find!" said Clementine, looking excited at the possibility.

"As long as we don't get zapped," said Raining.

"Or caught," Wilson said. "I don't think my mom would be very happy about that."

The four friends slipped quickly and quietly out of Dr. Kipper's office. With the place officially closed, the museum halls were eerily silent, and most of the lights had been shut off. Only a few emergency lights and the glowing red exit signs lit their way as they crept back into the exhibits.

"I bet the ghost hunters told them to leave all the lights off," Clementine whispered. "I've read that that's the only way ghosts will come out. They don't like electricity."

"Or they just want to keep everyone afraid," said Wilson, "so they can charge the museum as much as they want for their services."

"Leave me alone," Clementine said. "I'll believe what I want."

"Where should we start?" Amal asked, trying to get them to focus. "We all saw the big pterosaur fall. Should we start in the front? Or go check out one of the locations Lev mentioned for the other three 'haunting' incidents?"

"The front is probably crawling with maintenance workers by now," Wilson pointed out. "And besides, we already know those cables were clipped. I say we start with the Velociraptor."

"It won't be in the cafeteria anymore," said Raining.

"Then we're off to the theropod hall," said Wilson. "This way."

The four sleuths crept up the wide, central staircase toward the museum's second floor.

"Isn't the cafeteria in the basement?" said Clementine.

Wilson nodded. "Yeah, why?"

Clementine looked thoughtful. "I was just thinking that if someone moved the Velociraptor, they would've had to carry it down all these steps," she said. "Pretty hard work."

"Or they could have used the service elevator," Wilson said. "It's in the back near the offices."

"Hmm," said Clementine. "I suppose that's possible . . ."

The upper level of the museum was even quieter than the main floor had been.

"I guess the ghost hunters haven't finished exploring downstairs yet," Amal said. She led the way through the wide hallway, past darkened archways and dinosaur posters.

At the far end of the main corridor, two Troodon models, replete with feathers, flanked a slender, tall archway. They looked like ornately colored birds and were as tall as Clementine — and almost as brightly colored as her paint-splattered shirt and pants.

"There it is," said Wilson, picking up the pace and moving past Amal to lead the group. "The theropod hall."

The four sleuths stepped through the archway into the eerily lit exhibit. In the dim light, the theropod models cast long, flickering shadows across the enormous room.

"So, Wilson," said Amal. Her voice shook a little, but she tried hard not to sound scared. "What is a theropod, anyway? Aren't these just plain old dinosaurs?"

"It's kind of confusing," Wilson whispered as they prowled slowly through the display hall. "Theropods mainly walked on two legs, but they often had some feathers. And then later on, they evolved into birds. In fact, birds are theropods."

"Whoa," said Raining. "You mean the sparrows living in our eaves are dinosaurs?"

"Well, dinosaur cousins, anyway," Wilson said with a shrug. "But they are technically theropods."

Just then Wilson spotted the model of the Velociraptor skeleton. It stood near the farthest emergency exit, so it glowed red, making it extra creepy. "There it is," he said.

The four friends stood around the fearsome-looking model. It looked like an enormous sprinting bird with its long

neck and head lurched forward. The Velociraptor's lengthy tail pointed straight back behind it, helping to balance the creature as it ran. The dinosaur's arms were bent and close to its sides, the way a bird pulls in its wings, and its mouth was wide open, showing a maw full of sharp, curved teeth.

"Jeez, that's scary," Raining said, shuddering slightly. "I definitely would *not* want to see that thing chasing after me. So what do we do now? Dust for fingerprints or something?"

"I don't know if fingerprints will help," Wilson said. "Even if we knew how to get a good print off a model, we don't exactly have the police database of fingerprints to compare them to."

Clementine got as close to the model as the velvet rope allowed. "Did this thing have feathers too?" she asked.

"Yup," said Wilson.

Amal leaned back against the emergency exit door and yawned. "This is a waste of time," she said. "There's nothing here."

Suddenly, she yelped as the emergency door behind her opened and she fell back into an unlit cement hallway. "Ow!" Before she'd even hit the hard, cold floor of the hallway, red lights flashed, and a screeching siren wailed.

"Are you okay?" Clementine shouted, running to Amal's side. She helped her get to her feet, then pulled her back into the theropod hall. Together the two girls swung the heavy emergency door closed tight. But even with the door closed, the alarm kept screaming, and the lights kept flashing.

"Oh, no," Wilson said. "We're going to be in big trouble."

Just then, they heard loud, hurried footsteps — lots of them — coming from the second-floor's main hall. "It's coming from in there!" shouted an excited voice. "Bring the equipment!"

Flashlight beams suddenly swung into the room, nearly illuminating the four friends still gathered around the shrieking emergency exit.

"It's the ghost hunters!" Clementine whispered. She probably wanted to run over and join them.

"We have to get out of here," Wilson said. He looked around, but the only exit, other than the main archway, was the emergency door Amal had just stumbled upon.

Wilson took a deep breath and slammed the door open again. "Come on," he said. "Run!"

Beyond the door was a long, cold, cement hallway. Small lights positioned close to the floor provided the only light source.

"Where are we?" Raining asked, looking a little concerned.

"I don't know," Wilson admitted. "I've never been back here." He glanced around for a clue as to where they were, but the hallway stretched off in both directions with no markings besides a few glowing exit signs. "Let's try this way."

Wilson led them to the right, around a corner and past several unmarked black doors. The dimly lit hallway finally ended at a pair of heavy-looking, scraped-up red doors.

"Service elevator," Wilson said. He poked the down button. "We can get back to my mom's office from here. I know where this lets off on the first floor."

Wilson poked the button again and again, wishing it would hurry up. A moment later, the doors slid open, and the four of them stepped on.

Amal reached out to push the button for the first floor, but Wilson grabbed her wrist to stop her. "Wait a minute," he said. "I have an idea." Instead, he pushed the button marked "B" — for basement.

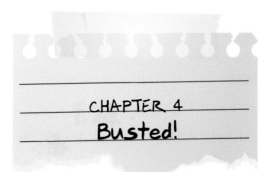

CHAPTER 4
Busted!

After a loud, slow ride, the elevator clunked to a stop on the lowest level of the museum. Wilson stepped slowly off, squinting into the unfamiliar darkness. This basement was nearly pitch black.

"Where are we?" Raining whispered, stepping off the elevator behind him. "Other than the basement, I mean."

"I don't know," said Wilson. "Put your hand on my shoulder so we don't get separated."

Raining did. It helped to know his friend was right there with him. "Clementine, Amal," Wilson said. "Form a chain."

Together, the four friends moved slowly into the darkness. Wilson's eyes were gradually becoming accustomed to the lack of light, and soon he saw little spots scattered all over, as if tiny specks were reflecting off hundreds of things in the room.

Suddenly Wilson bumped into something hard and cold, and there was a loud clatter of metal as whatever he'd hit crashed to the ground.

"Shh!" said Amal.

"Sorry!" said Wilson. "I walked into something."

"I sort of guessed that," Amal said wryly.

"There's good news, though," Wilson said. "I know where we are now, and at least part of the mystery is solved."

"Care to let the rest of us in on it?" Clementine said from the back of the group.

Wilson didn't have to say a word, though. A moment later he pushed open a swinging door, and they stepped into a room flooded with green-tinted sunlight coming through the window wells in the courtyard.

"The cafeteria," Wilson said. "The service elevator must open into it. So now we know how the Velociraptor got down here."

Clementine nodded. "Yup," she said, putting her hands on her hips. "It took the service elevator. Smart dinosaur."

Wilson rolled his eyes. "You mean someone put it on a dolly and wheeled it onto the elevator," he said.

"Or that," Clementine admitted with a shrug.

"Okay," said Amal, stepping between Clementine and Wilson, "so someone brought the dino down here on the service elevator. But who?"

"Who would want to?" asked Raining.

"You know what they always say about solving a mystery," Amal said, hopping up on the edge of a cafeteria table. "Follow the money."

Raining, Clementine, and Wilson all took seats at the table around Amal.

"I don't understand how fake ghost sightings would make anyone any money, though," Clementine said.

The friends sat in silence for a few moments, thinking, but no one else seemed to have any ideas either.

"I guess we'd better head back to my mom's office," Wilson finally said, standing up. "She might be done with her meeting with the psychics by now. And I don't want her to get back and realize we're not there."

The others sighed and got to their feet as well. They all headed through the main cafeteria doors, but they'd barely taken a few steps when they heard excited whispers from around the corner.

"Shh," Wilson said. He quickly ushered his friends back into the cafeteria, and they stood by the door to listen. A moment later, they heard a girl's voice, followed by the laughter of more girls.

"It's Ruthie Rothchild!" Clementine said. "I'd recognize that voice anywhere."

Amal clapped her hand over Clementine's mouth to silence her. "Keep it down. Let's see what she's up to."

"There won't be anyone in there," Ruthie was saying as the small group of girls approached. "We can take as much

ice cream from the freezer as we can carry!"

"Yeah," said another voice — Ruthie's friend Sloan. "Then we can sell them to the people waiting out front."

The four sleuths hurried away from the cafeteria door as the girls' voices drew closer. "Back in the kitchen," Wilson hissed. "Quick."

The others followed him, and they pushed through the swinging doors to the kitchen, then huddled together behind a metal cabinet where they wouldn't be seen. "Once they grab the goodies," Wilson said, "we'll jump out. Catch them red-handed."

Clementine nodded and smiled. Wilson knew how pleased she would be to get Ruthie in big trouble for something like this. And if Ruthie had anything to do with the haunting, it would make Clementine's day. The two girls had known each other since they were young, and they didn't exactly get along.

Amal peeked carefully around the cabinet and watched as Ruthie and her gang pushed open the swinging doors and headed straight for the big industrial freezer.

"They're going in there now," Amal said. "It's Sloan and Ruthie and that new girl from school. Sierra, I think her name is Sierra."

"She sure made friends with the wrong group," Clementine said, shaking her head.

"Okay," said Amal. "They're opening the freezer. Ruthie has a big bag to carry the ice cream."

"So it's pre-meditated," Wilson said. "She planned this."

"They're filling it up," Amal said.

"That must be like fifty ice cream bars and Popsicles and cones!" Clementine said. "Oh, they are so done for." She leapt out from their hiding place, and the four of them sprinted over to the ice-cream-thieving girls before they even knew what was happening.

"Busted!" Clementine said, snatching the bag out of Ruthie's hand.

Ruthie rolled her eyes. "Fine," she said. "You caught us. Put the ice cream back and we'll leave."

"Oh, no," said Amal, stepping right up to Ruthie. "You're not walking away from this. We're going to tell Lev."

"Oh, please," said Sloan. "That nitwit is so caught up with this haunting stuff, he won't care about some dumb ice cream. Besides, we'll deny it. It'll be your word against ours. Why would he believe you?"

"Maybe because my mom works here," Wilson said.

"Exactly," Clementine said, looking pleased. "Like I said, busted."

Ruthie didn't respond. She didn't even look at Clementine. "Come on, you two," she said to her friends. "Let's go. It's not like they can arrest us." She and Sloan strutted across the cafeteria. But the new girl, Sierra, hesitated.

"Want to say something?" Amal asked.

The new girl opened her mouth to speak, but Ruthie called from the doorway, "Come on, Sierra. You don't have to talk to them."

"If you guys had anything to do with the weird stuff going on here," Wilson said quickly, "you can tell us. We know it was all Ruthie's idea."

"Sierra!" Ruthie snapped.

If the new girl had wanted to say something, she didn't anymore. She hurried after Ruthie and Sloan as they left the cafeteria.

"What was that about?" Amal said.

"I don't know. She seemed like she wanted to tell us something," Wilson said.

"Maybe she's not as awful as Ruthie and Sloan," Clementine said, taking a step toward the cafeteria doors. "Maybe she feels bad for getting messed up with those two criminals."

"And maybe they *are* involved in what's been going on here," Amal said, pressing her hands together. "Maybe she wanted to confess. Maybe she wanted to tell us everything!"

Wilson bit his lip. It didn't seem quite right. How would Ruthie and her friends have gotten the Velociraptor moved and the Quetzalcoatlus to fall?

"Let's head to my mom's office," he said. "She'll be back soon."

CHAPTER 5
Mr. Moonstar

Dr. Kipper's office was empty when they got there, but not for long. The four of them had hardly taken their seats when Dr. Kipper swept into the room — and she wasn't alone.

Before anyone could say anything, a man wearing a long, silvery robe and an array of colorful beaded necklaces trailed into the office after her. Mr. Collini followed closely behind. "Here they are, Mr. Moonstar," he said, waving toward the kids on the couch.

"What's going on?" Wilson asked, looking back and forth between the grown-ups.

"Kids," said Mr. Collini, "this is Mr. Moonstar. He's the psychic who's been investigating what's been happening here at the museum. Since you were all right there when the Quetzalcoatlus fell, I thought it might be helpful if he spoke with you. You can tell him about your spiritual experience at the time of the incident."

"'Spiritual experience'?" Amal repeated, raising an eyebrow.

"Do we have to?" Wilson asked, looking at his mother.

Dr. Kipper sighed, but she nodded gently. "Let's just consider it a favor to the museum," she said with a smile.

Wilson knew what his mom really meant. She thought it was silly — and probably a waste of time — but Mr. Collini wanted it. And with the museum director's reputation for having a bad temper, it was best to do what he wanted.

"Ugh!" Amal grumbled, slouching back on the couch. "This is so silly."

Wilson leaned close to his friend. "Remember what happened to Dr. Lin," he said. "Let's just get it over with."

Dr. Lin, the museum's former head of paleontology, had been fired only a few weeks before. Wilson and his friends had all been in the prehistoric mammals exhibit when it happened. It seemed that Dr. Lin hadn't agreed with Mr. Collini's ideas about how to dress the early humans in a display of mammoths. Dr. Lin had wanted it to be accurate; Mr. Collini had wanted it to be exciting. It was that difference in opinions that had led to Dr. Lin's departure.

Thankfully, the interview didn't take long. Mr. Moonstar asked about any chills they might have felt before the model fell. Then he asked if any of them had been visited by ghosts lately, or ever. Only Clementine had a story for that question. Mr. Moonstar was *very* interested, even though it had happened five years earlier when Clementine and her mother had visited some old churches in Venice during a family trip to Italy.

"Do you think it might have something to do with this?" Clementine said, leaning forward on the couch eagerly.

"All things are connected," Mr. Moonstar said, clasping his hands together in front of his face, "in the spirit world."

"Whoa . . ." said Clementine. She was easily impressed by talk like that.

When he was done, Mr. Moonstar bowed to them and left. Mr. Collini hurried down the hallway after the psychic, peppering him with questions about the kids and whether any of them might be responsible for the haunting.

Dr. Kipper looked exhausted as she checked the time. "They're opening the cafeteria so employees and anyone else stuck inside the museum during this fiasco can have lunch," she said. "Why don't you four go and find something to eat?"

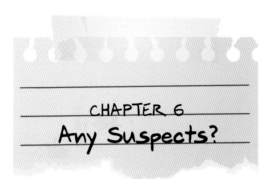

CHAPTER 6
Any Suspects?

As the four friends walked to the cafeteria, they discussed the case and what they knew so far.

"Do we have any suspects?" Amal asked.

"Besides the spirit of a long-dead pterodactyl mother?" Clementine said with a laugh. "How about Ruthie and company?"

Wilson wasn't so sure. "Remember what Amal said," he reminded his friends. "It's the key to most mysteries: follow the money."

"So who makes money from the museum closing?" Raining said. "Certainly not Mr. Collini."

"That's a good point," said Wilson. In his mind, he crossed Mr. Collini off the suspect list.

"But, Wilson," Clementine interjected, "Ruthie was going to make money! Don't you remember? She and her friends were going to sell the ice cream they stole from the cafeteria to people waiting out front to get back in."

"That's true," Amal agreed thoughtfully.

Clementine grinned. Wilson could tell she was hoping this would be the perfect chance to bust Ruthie for something big.

"We should check it out," Wilson conceded. "But I don't know if she had the opportunity to pull all the tricks Lev told us about."

"Not to mention dropping that huge quetzl-what-do-you-call-it from the ceiling like that," Raining said.

The cafeteria was buzzing when they walked in. All the scientists and staff, all the ghost hunters, even Mr. Collini was there, and everyone was yapping about ghosts they'd seen.

Every table was full, but Wilson spotted Ruthie, Sloan, and Sierra in the far corner, sitting in a little circle. "There they are," he said.

"Let's see if we can get Sierra alone," Clementine said. "I think she wants to confess."

"I'll take care of it," Amal said. She strode right up to the three girls and said, "Sierra. The head of security wants to talk to you."

"Me?" Sierra said, looking worried. She glanced over at Ruthie for help.

Ruthie just rolled her eyes. "Well, tell him we don't want to talk to him," she snapped.

"Well, lucky for you, he just wants Sierra," Amal said. "He's waiting outside the cafeteria."

Sierra looked at Ruthie again, then at Sloan, but the other girls just shrugged. Reluctantly, Sierra got up and followed Amal into the hall. Clementine, Wilson, and Raining all trailed close behind them.

When they exited the cafeteria, Sierra glanced around the empty hallway. "Where — hey, what is this?" she said. She grabbed for the doors to go back inside, but Amal blocked her.

"We know Ruthie's been up to no good," Clementine said. "We know it's not your fault. We don't want you to get in trouble for her."

"So why don't you tell us what she's been doing?" Amal said.

Sierra looked confused. "Huh? But you already stopped her. Don't you remember?" she said. "We were going to steal some ice cream?"

"Yeah," said Clementine slowly, "but what else? Wasn't Ruthie behind all the weird ghost stuff that's been happening?"

"What?" Sierra said. She shook her head. "No. That's ridiculous. Didn't you see all the ghost hunters and the psychic running around? This isn't some practical joke. It's the real deal."

"Oh, come on," said Amal, rolling her eyes.

"Look," Sierra said, pulling her phone from her pocket. She poked around and then held it up to show off a local news website. The entire page was covered with headlines about the museum — especially about Mr. Moonstar.

"See?" Sierra said. "Everyone's saying it's real. Mr. Moonstar is getting, like, totally famous."

"Wait, I'm confused," Raining said. "Didn't you want to tell us something before?"

"Like that Ruthie has been behind all this?" Amal suggested.

"No," said Sierra, shaking her head. "I wanted to tell you she was bad news — way worse than I thought. I didn't think I wanted to be friends with her and Sloan anymore. I was hoping I could hang out with you guys instead."

"Oh," said Amal.

"That makes sense," said Clementine. "Do you still want to?"

Sierra shrugged one shoulder. "I don't know," she said. "You guys are being pretty weird. Besides, Ruthie's mom drove me down here. I should at least take the ride home, right?" With that, she slipped back into the cafeteria.

CHAPTER 7
Ghost Hunters

"Well, that was a dead end," Wilson said a few minutes later. He took a bite from his hot dog as he walked. They'd each gotten one. It was the only thing they could grab and take with them.

"Still," Clementine said, "at least she's not as horrible as Ruthie, right?"

"I guess," Wilson said. "But she also gave us other important info — Mr. Moonstar."

"What about him?" Raining asked, sounding confused.

"I get it," Amal said. "Follow the money. Moonstar's doing very well today. His team of ghost hunters are getting paid to be here, and he's probably getting the most fame he's ever seen."

"Exactly," said Wilson. "Let's see if we can track him down. I didn't see him in the cafeteria."

It took quite a while to find Mr. Moonstar. The four of them wandered the wide, echoing halls as lunchtime ended and the lights went off, signifying that the ghost hunt was on again.

"Great," said Clementine sarcastically. "So the lights are off, and now the dinosaur spirits will find us."

"Hopefully the ghost hunters will," said Amal. "That's probably the fastest way to find Moonstar in this humungous place."

As it turned out, she was right. As the four sleuths turned a corner, they were nearly blinded by four super-bright flashlights.

"Who's there?" one of the ghost hunters shouted. They hurried down the hall and surrounded the kids. They all carried flashlights and special goggles, plus big, heavy-looking backpacks with antennae sticking out all over the place.

"Just a bunch of kids," said the lead ghost hunter.

"Just a bunch of ghost hunters," Amal retorted.

"Have you found any poltergeists yet?" Clementine asked.

"The investigation is still in progress," said one of the hunters. "And we only report to Mr. Moonstar."

"Of course," said Wilson. "And where *is* Mr. Moonstar?"

"He's still doing interviews," one of the ghost hunters said. "Check Collini's office."

"He's interviewing Collini?" Wilson asked.

"Nah," said the hunter. "Collini was his first interview. No spiritual involvement there at all. This interview is with some doctor who used to work here. I think he was in charge of the dinosaur exhibit or something. We found him skulking around in the pterosaur exhibit."

Wilson could hardly believe it. This could be a great lead. "You mean Dr. Lin?" he said. "He's here?"

"That sounds right," said the hunter. "Now if you'll excuse us, we still have a lot of ground to cover."

The group of ghost hunters hurried away, and Wilson turned to his friends. "Maybe money isn't the issue after all," he said. "Maybe it's revenge."

CHAPTER 8
A New Suspect

"Dr. Lin?" Wilson said as the former head of paleontology finally stepped out of Mr. Collini's office.

Wilson and his friends had been waiting just outside the closed door for almost thirty minutes hoping to run into the man.

Dr. Lin's interview with Mr. Moonstar must have been a lot tougher than ours, Wilson thought.

"Wilson Kipper!" Dr. Lin said with a big smile. He sure didn't seem to be feeling angry or vengeful — at all. "How are you doing? I haven't seen you in quite some time."

"Um, I'm good, thanks," said Wilson. "How about you?" He'd always liked Dr. Lin. The former head paleontologist had always been great about not treating Wilson like a little kid.

Dr. Lin shook his head gravely. "I'm okay. I wish I could say the same for the museum. Sure is some weird stuff happening down here today, huh?" he said.

"Does Mr. Moonstar think you're involved?" Clementine asked. "Spiritually, I mean."

Dr. Lin grinned. "He might!" he said. "I have no idea. He's a . . . hard man to read."

"Dr. Lin," Wilson said. "I don't want to be rude, but I have to ask you. Why are you here today? Didn't Mr. Collini — I mean . . ."

"Yes, I was fired," Dr. Lin admitted sadly. "And trust me when I tell you that being back here isn't easy. It brings back a lot of memories. But Wilson, you know better than anyone — what has my number-one obsession always been?"

Wilson knew because it was the same as his. "Pterosaurs," he said.

Dr. Lin nodded and smiled. "I couldn't miss the grand opening of the new exhibit," he said. "After all, your mother and I worked very hard to make it so special."

"That's true," Wilson said. He realized it had been silly to think Dr. Lin would be involved with anything so harmful to the museum's exhibits. He'd always taken such great care of them when he worked there.

"I came by for the opening, and when they locked the front doors I knew Lev would start questioning everyone out front," Dr. Lin explained. "So instead of heading outside, I hurried deeper into the museum, thinking I could find someplace to hide till this blew over."

Wilson assumed that plan hadn't gone very well given that Dr. Lin had just left a lengthy interview with the head ghost hunter.

Dr. Lin shook his head. "Not my best idea," he admitted. "I should have thought it through. When Mr. Moonstar's ghost hunters found me, they thought I was up to no good."

"You can't blame them. That does sort of make sense," Amal said.

Dr. Lin shrugged. "I haven't done anything wrong, so I suppose we'll just have to wait and see what conclusions they come to," he said. "Anyway, it was nice to see you, Wilson." With a wave goodbye, the doctor headed off down the hall.

"Well, at least that's one suspect eliminated. But that still leaves Moonstar," Raining said.

The four kids stepped into Collini's office and found Mr. Moonstar sitting on the carpet with his eyes closed and his legs crossed.

"Do you think he's asleep?" Raining whispered.

"He's meditating," Clementine said, leaning down to look into the psychic's peaceful-looking face. "At least I think that's what he's doing."

Just then, the phone on Mr. Collini's desk started ringing. It rang and rang. More lights lit up on the phone. It seemed like every line in the museum was ringing at the same time.

"Doesn't he hear that?" Amal said. She waved a hand back and forth in front of Mr. Moonstar, and the psychic smiled a little, even though he never opened his eyes.

"I hear all," Mr. Moonstar said in a calm, monotone voice. "Alas, it is not my phone."

"That's true," said Wilson. "It's Mr. Collini's." He stepped up to the desk, cleared his throat, and picked up the still-ringing phone.

"What are you doing?" Clementine said urgently. "Let it ring!"

Wilson shook his head, punched the button for line one, and said in his deepest and most serious voice, "This is Mr. Collini."

After a few moments of listening quietly, Wilson hung up the phone. He grinned at his friends and said, "I think we have a new suspect."

CHAPTER 9

Cracking the Case

"I don't get it," said Raining as the four friends hurried down the main steps of the museum. "Who was on the phone?"

"Reporters," Wilson said, glancing back over his shoulder at his friends. "TV news, websites, local networks, and national cable networks."

"And that made you decide Moonstar isn't behind this?" Amal asked. "I'm with Raining — I don't get it."

Amal and Raining sounded confused, but Clementine was nodding in understanding. "He never really made sense as a suspect," she said. "Even if he had cut the cables on the Quetzalcoatlus, he certainly wasn't around last week to flicker the lights and drag a dinosaur skeleton halfway across the museum just to spook Lev."

"Exactly," said Wilson. "But one person had both the opportunity *and* the motive for all the alleged ghost acts — Mr. Collini."

"Mr. Collini?" Amal said. "But what was *his* motive?"

"Don't you see?" Wilson said as the four swung around the staircase and hurried to the big front room. "This is great publicity for the museum."

They reached the front and found Dr. Kipper, Mr. Collini, and Lev standing in the now–empty center of the room. The remains of the Quetzlcoatlus and the Allosaurus — its first victim in more than sixty million years — had been cleared away.

"Wilson," Dr. Kipper said, "what are you four doing here? Did you have some lunch?"

"Yeah, we did," Wilson said. "Hey, Mr. Collini, I was wondering, how did promotion go for the new pterosaur exhibit?"

"It went fine," said Mr. Collini. "Why do you ask?"

"I don't remember seeing anything about it in the paper," Amal said.

"There was a small article," Dr. Kipper pointed out. "I remember seeing it in *The Daily Post*."

"Ah, yes," said Mr. Collini, frowning. But he brightened quickly and waved his arms toward the crowd still waiting outside in the summer heat. "But look! It worked wonders. Look at the crowd out there."

"You think they're here for the pterosaurs?" Lev asked. He shook his head. "I think it's the ghosts that are bringing them out today." He turned to the kids. "That's exactly what that woman told us this morning, remember?"

"Ha!" Mr. Collini laughed nervously. "That's ridiculous. If they wanted ghosts they'd wait till Halloween."

"You think so?" Wilson said suspiciously.

Mr. Collini didn't reply. Instead, he checked his watch. "I should really be getting back to my office," he muttered, starting off.

Amal grabbed his arm to stop him. "Mr. Collini," she said. "Do you have a key to all the emergency exits in the building?"

"Well, of course I do," he replied. "But why — "

"Then the alarms wouldn't go off if you used an emergency door," Wilson continued.

"And of course you have access to the catwalk above us right now?" Clementine said.

"Naturally I do, but — " Mr. Collini started to say.

"You must work some very long hours, too," Raining interrupted him. "You're probably here all the time. Even when there are only a couple of security guards roaming the halls, maybe someone from the cleaning crew?"

Mr. Collini opened his mouth to speak, but nothing came out.

"What are you kids getting at?" said Lev.

Wilson didn't have to answer. He could see the gears turning in Lev's mind, and a moment later, Lev turned to Mr. Collini.

"Hey, wait a minute," he said. *"You're* the ghost, aren't you?"

"Mr. Collini!" Dr. Kipper said, looking horrified. "Is that true?"

Mr. Collini didn't speak, but his cheeks turned red.

"I can't believe this!" Dr. Kipper exclaimed. "You destroyed our Quetzalcoatlus and Allosaurus models! You could have seriously hurt someone!"

"Please understand!" Mr. Collini said. "I never intended to hurt anyone. I never even meant to break anything! I only cut one cable. I thought the giant thing would soar across the lobby like it had come back to life."

"But why?" Dr. Kipper asked.

"Publicity!" Mr. Collini said. "I'm no scientist, Carolyn. My job is to bring in the money. And for money, we need visitors."

Lev shook his head and pulled the set of handcuffs from his belt. "I'm sorry, Mr. Collini," he said. "But this is a matter for the Capitol City police."

"I know, I know," said Mr. Collini. For a moment he looked upset, but when he caught sight of the crowds milling around outside, waiting to come in, he smiled again. "But look at all the people! It worked! The museum will have its best day in years."

With that, Lev led him away, toward the security room, to wait for the police.

"See?" Amal whispered to her friends. "I told you — follow the money."

"There's still one thing I don't understand, though," Clementine said. "What about the giant flying ghost Lev saw?"

Wilson stepped behind the front desk. He had a feeling he'd find what he wanted, and he did — a big, heavy flashlight like the ones the security team carried. Right next to it sat a small plastic model of a pterosaur.

Wilson clicked on the flashlight, held up the pterosaur toy, and cast its shadow on the far wall. It was huge. "Easy," he said, grinning at Clementine. "Now let's see if we can get the lights turned back on. I still want to check out the pterosaur exhibit before closing time."

Steve B.

About the Author

Steve Brezenoff is the author of more than fifty middle-grade chapter books, including the Field Trip Mysteries series, the Ravens Pass series of thrillers, and the Return to Titanic series. In his spare time, he enjoys video games, cycling, and cooking. Steve lives in Minneapolis with his wife, Beth, and their son and daughter.

Lisa W.

About the Illustrator

Lisa K. Weber is an illustrator currently living in Oakland, California. She graduated from Parsons School of Design in 2000 and then began freelancing. Since then, she has completed many print, animation, and design projects, including graphic novelizations of classic literature, character and background designs for children's cartoons, and textiles for dog clothing.

GLOSSARY

confess (kuhn-FES) — to admit something, usually something you did that was wrong

exhibit (eg-ZIB-it) — a public display or show

motive (MOH-tiv) — the reason why a person did something

paleontologist (pale-ee-uhn-TOL-uh-jist) — a scientist who studies fossils and other ancient life

poltergeist (POHL-ter-gahyst) — a ghost that makes its presence known through noises or by moving objects around

psychic (SAHY-kik) — a person who claims to sense supernatural forces

publicity (puh-BLIS-i-tee) — information about a person or event meant to draw people's attention and get them interested

revenge (ri-VENJ) — the act of getting back at someone for injuring or harming you or someone you care about

skeptical (SKEP-ti-kuhl) — not believing that something or someone is truthful

sleuth (SLOOTH) — someone who solves mysteries or is good at finding out facts

DISCUSSION QUESTIONS

1. Which dinosaur was your favorite? Talk about your reasoning.

2. Who did you think was going to be behind the strange events at the museum? Discuss why you thought that person was guilty.

2. Mr. Collini thought the only good way to advertise the exhibit was to make up a story about a ghost. Can you think of any better ways to advertise? Talk about how you would let people know about the new exhibit.

WRITING PROMPTS

1. Imagine you discovered a new dinosaur. Write a paragraph about what it looks like, what it eats, and what makes it special.

2. Imagine that there really was a ghost in the museum. Write a paragraph describing how the story would be different.

3. Sierra wasn't comfortable with Ruthie and the other girls stealing ice cream. Have your friends ever tried to make you do something that you didn't want to do? Write about your experience. Explain what you did and why.

NATURAL HISTORY INFORMATION

The National Museum of Natural History (NMNH), which opened in Washington, D.C. in 1910, is one of the most visited museums in the world. It is home to more than 126 million artifacts — the largest natural history collection in the world! The museum welcomes more than eight million people each year and is dedicated to educating visitors about nature and cultures around the world.

The NMNH has seven departments of research:

- **anthropology** — the study of humankind
- **botany** — the study of plants
- **entomology** — the study of insects
- **invertebrate zoology** — the study of animals without a backbone
- **mineral sciences** — explores gems, volcanoes, rocks, minerals, and meteorites
- **paleobiology** — the study of fossilized animals and plants
- **vertebrate zoology** — the study of animals with a backbone

DINOSAUR FACTS

Richard Owen, a British paleontologist, invented the word "dinosaur" in 1842. He combined the Greek words "deinos" (awe-inspiring) and "sauros" (lizard) to form "dinosaur."

Dinosaurs lived from 230 million to 65 million years ago in what is called the **Mesozoic Era**. The Mesozoic Era is broken into three periods: the **Triassic**, **Jurassic**, and the **Cretaceous**.

Capable of growing throughout their whole life, dinosaurs could get very large. The longest dinosaur ever found is the **Seismosaurus** at 100 feet long, the tallest is the **Brachiosaurus** at 40 feet, and the heaviest is the **Argentinosaurus** at around 80 tons.

Dinosaurs are often put into one of two groups: herbivores and carnivores. **Herbivores** only ate plants and **carnivores** only ate meat. If a dinosaur had flat teeth, it was most likely a herbivore. If it had curved, pointed, or serrated teeth, it was most likely a carnivore.